the 4 disciples

IN DEDICATION TO:
MY KIDS MALACHI SWINEA + EMERIE SWINEA.
ALSO, IN HOPES THAT
MY COMIC BOOK CAN HAVE
A POSITIVE IMPACT ON **THE WORLD.**

the 4 disciples

PRESENTS

TFD SHORT SKITS VOL.1
Spring Break Time

TFD SHORT SKITS VOL.1   #1
Spring Break Time

TFD SHORT SKITS VOL.2   #2
Coming soon! June, 2017

TFD SHORT SKITS VOL.3   #3
Coming soon! August, 2017

the 4 disciples

EDITOR IN CHIEF: ADIVA PETERS

CHIEF CREATIVE OFFICER: JUSTIN SWINEA

DIGITAL PRODUCTION: ANA KARENINA, JOSHUA ISRAEL, ARIEL VIOLA, OSIRIS SANTOS, RON HUBBARD, JERMALE THOMAS

DIRECTOR OF COMMUNICATION: JUSTIN SWINEA

PUBLISHER: COMPASS PRINTING PLUS

©2017 JUSTIN SWINEA THE 4 DISCIPLES (TFD), INC. ALL RIGHTS RESERVED. ALL CHARACTERS FEATURED IN THIS ISSUE AND THE DISTINCTIVE NAMES AND LIKENESSES THEREOF, AND ALL RELATED INDICIA ARE TRADEMARKS OF THE 4 DISCIPLES (ALSO KNOWN AS TFD) CHARACTERS, INC. NO SIMILARITY BETWEEN ANY OF THE NAMES, CHARACTER'S, PERSON'S AND/OR INSTITUTIONS IN THIS MAGAZINE WITH THOSE OF ANY LIVING OR DEAD PERSON OR INSTITUTION IS INTENDED, AND ANY SUCH SIMILARITY THAT MAY EXIST IS PURELY COINCEDENTAL.

VEREDAI

the 4 disciples

the 4 disciples

SPRING BREAK'S OUT

continue to story

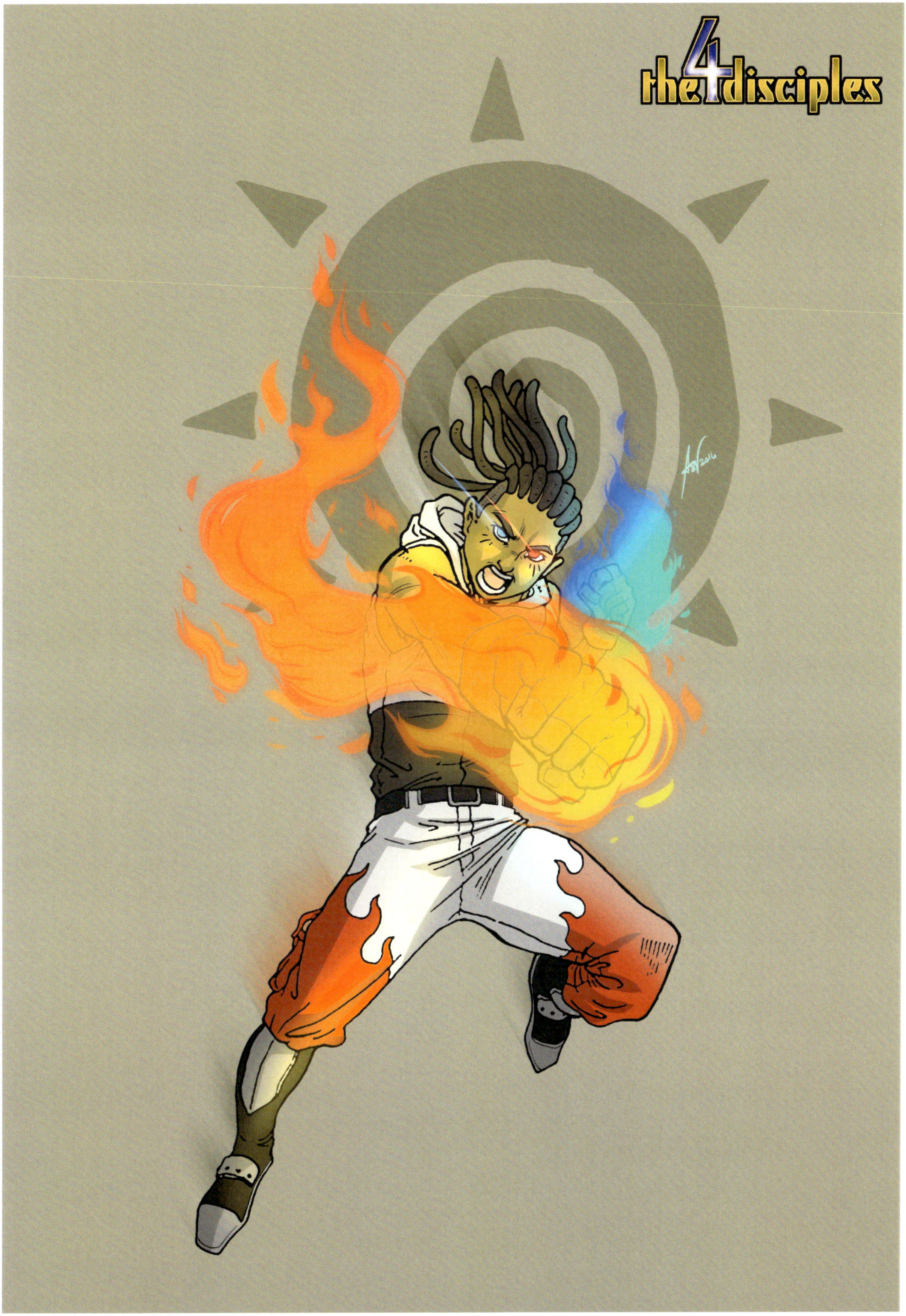
the 4 disciples

SPRING BREAK'S OUT

continue to story

The Invincible Fly

continue to story

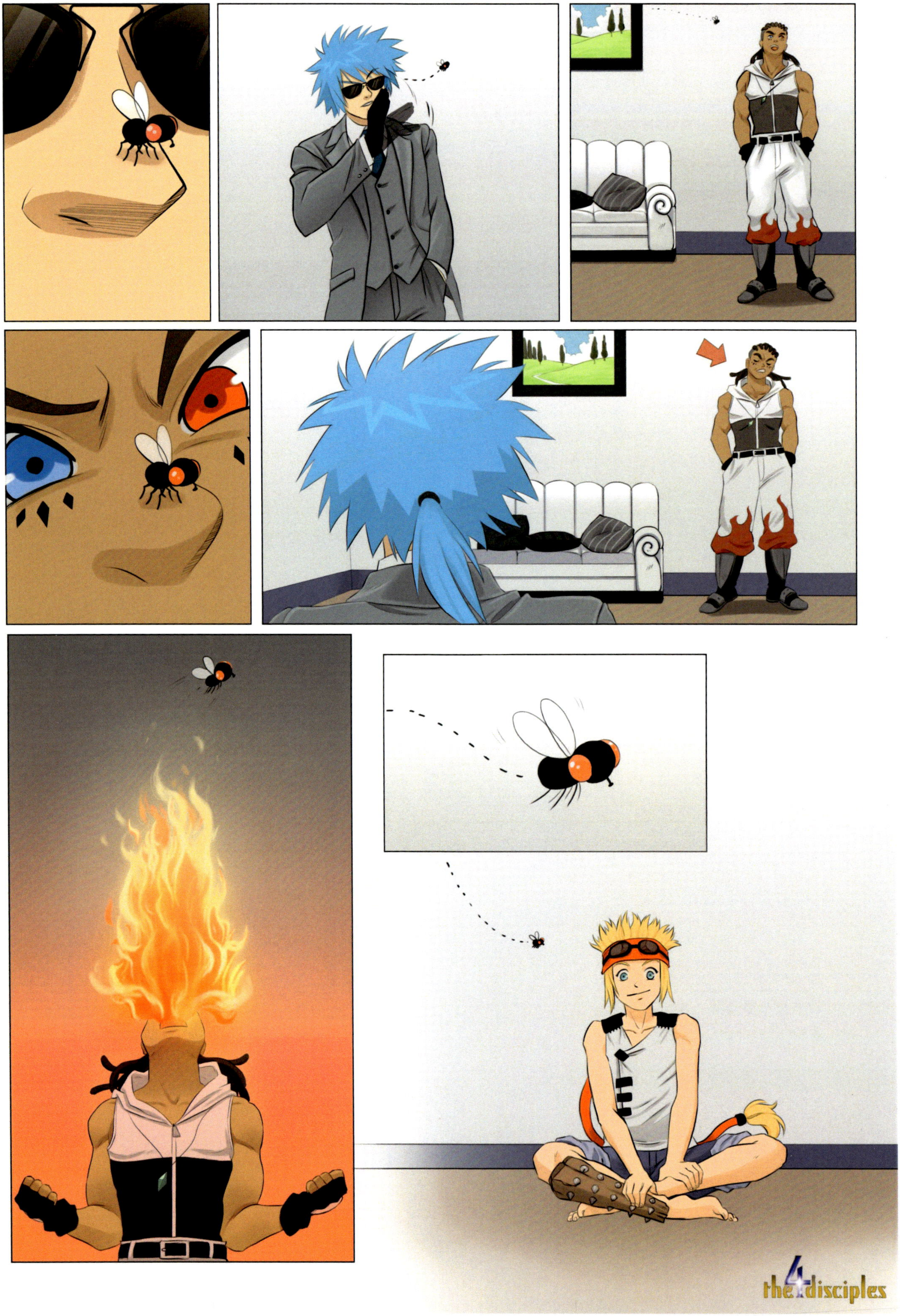

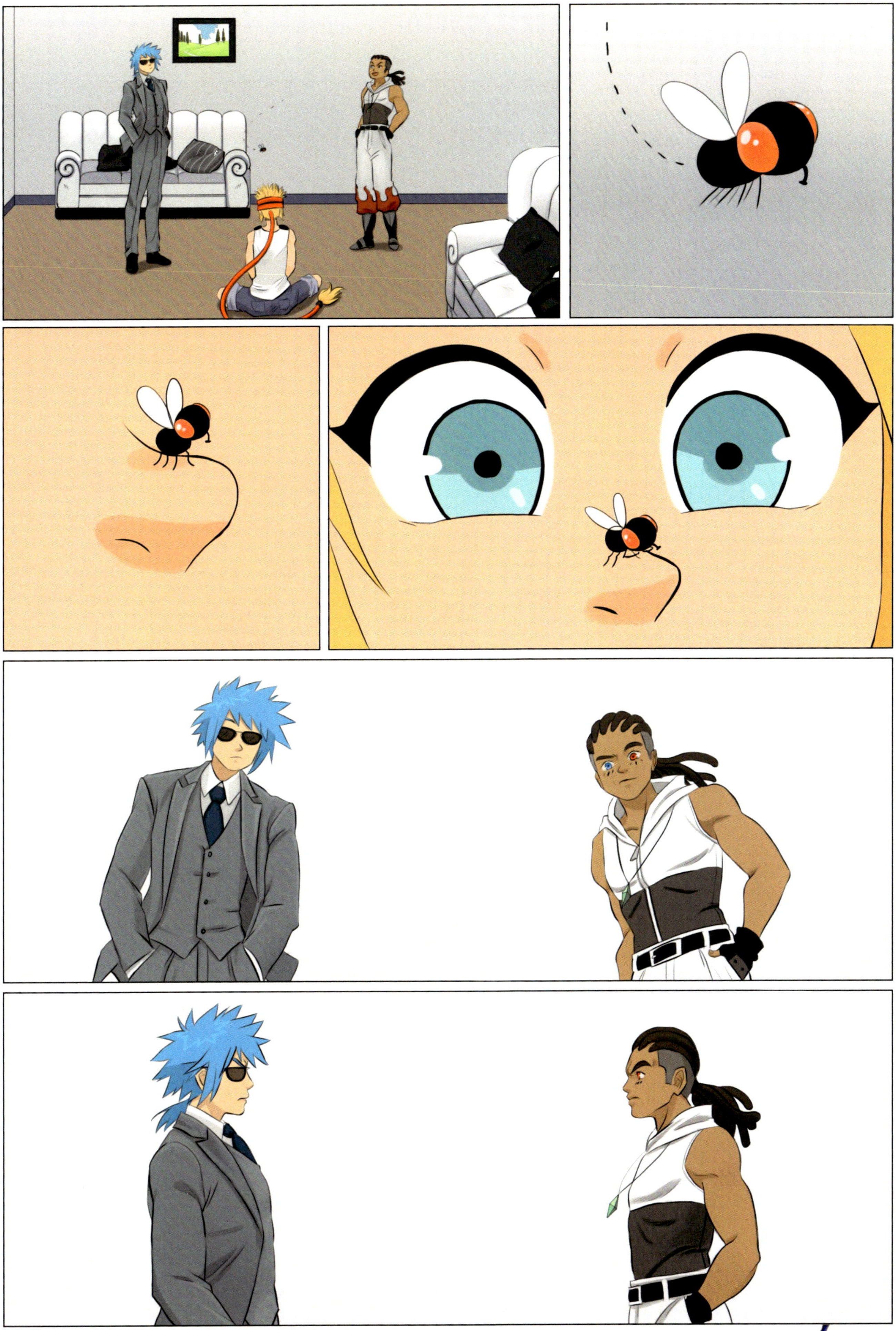

WWAZAMMMMM!

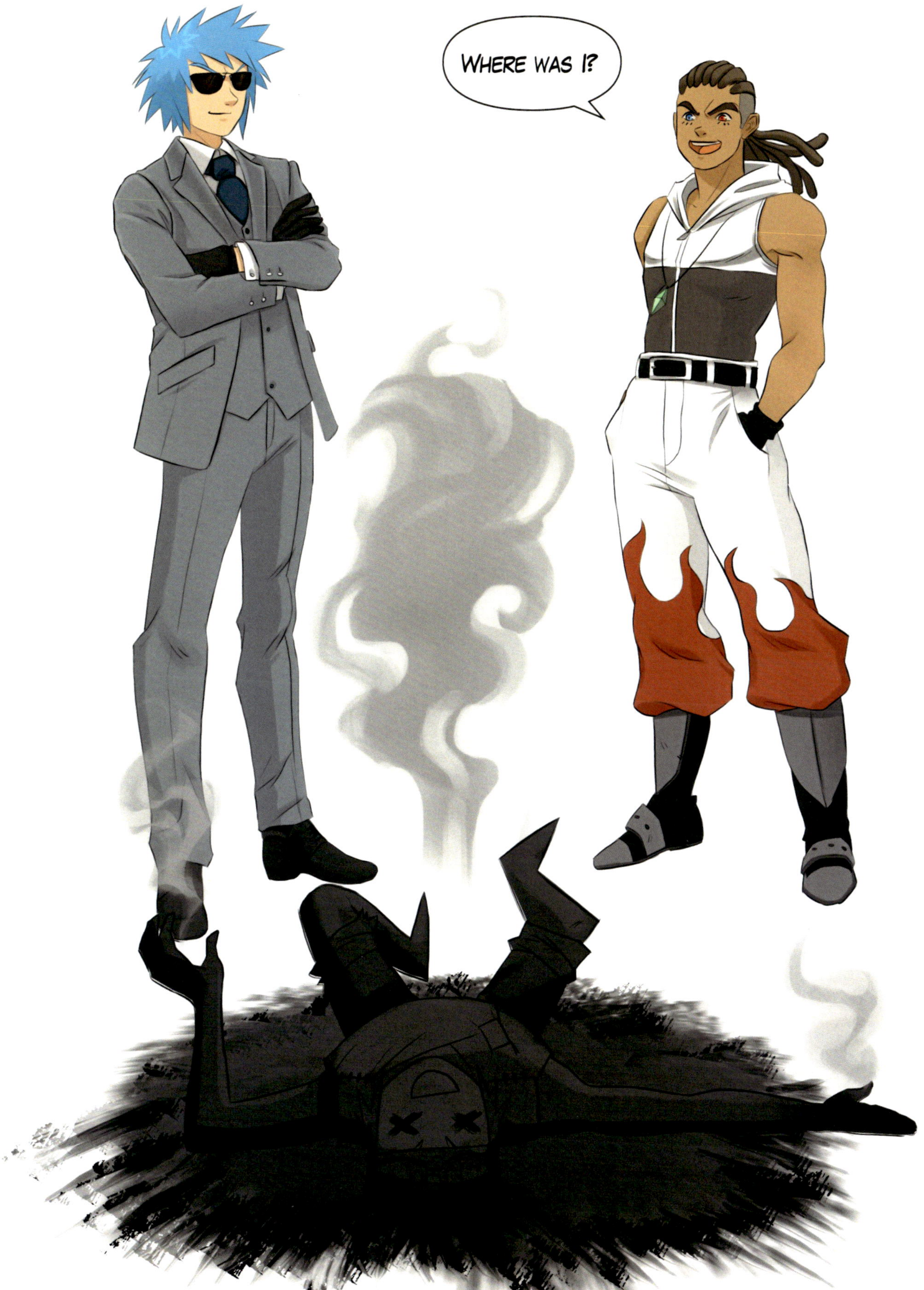

the4disciples

the 4 disciples

POLICE REPORT

NAME: LEUCETIUS
AGE: 25
HEIGHT: 6'3
BIRTH CITY: TROY NEW YORK
BIO: OLDER TWIN BROTHER OF BARAK. FORMER MEMBER OF THE ASSASINATION TASK FORCE AND SPECIAL OPS UNIT (S.P.U.). NOW, BODY GUARDS FOR HIRE. LEUCETIUS AND BARAK ARE KNOWN AS THUNDER AND LIGHTNING TWINS AND SHOULD BE UNDER HEAVY WATCH

April Fool's

continue to story

HEY GUYS!
IT'S ME AGAIN, VEREDAI, FROM THE 4 DISCIPLES.
WE REALLY NEED YOUR HELP IN SUPPORTING THE 4 DISCIPLES COMIC BOOK. IF YOU DON'T HELP US,
ME AND MY BROTHERS ARE GOING TO GET SICK AND STARVE TO DEATH.
GET OVER HEREEEEE!
NOW I GOT YOU!
HA-HA-HAAAA!
FOODDDD!
I NEED FOODD NOWWWWWWW!
GREAT!
I'M ON MY LAST MARSHMALLOW, NOW WHAT AM I GOING TO DO?
APRIL FOOLS!
WE'RE NOT STARVING!
BUT WE COULD SURE USE YOUR SUPPORT BY GOING AHEAD AND CLICKING THE LINK BELOW OR ABOVE US.
SO GO AHEAD AND LIKE, LOVE, SHARE OR COMMENT,
AND TELL YOUR FRIENDS ABOUT THE 4 DISCIPLES COMIC BOOK.
WELL, THAT'S ALL FOR NOW GUYS! AND UNTIL WE MEET AGAIN,
PEACE BE WITH YOU!

VEREDAI

the 4 disciples

POLICE REPORT

NAME: Veredai
AGE: 14
HEIGHT: 6'2
BIRTH PLANET: Zalea
POWERS+ABILITIES: POWERS, UNCONFIRMED. ABILITIES, SUPER STRENGTH

Guess Who?

continue to story

EEEKK... EEEKK...

WOOAH!!!

VEREDAI! VEREDAI!! ...

SHK...

LOOK!

THAT LADY'S HAIR IS SO PRETTY AND LONG LIKE MINE!

EXCUSE ME!, MA'AM.

I JUST WANTED TO SAY HOW MUCH I LOVE YOUR PRETTY LONG HAIR.

WELL, GO TELL HER SHE HAS NICE HAIR THEN, I'M SURE SHE WILL APPRECIATE IT.

TAP..TAP...

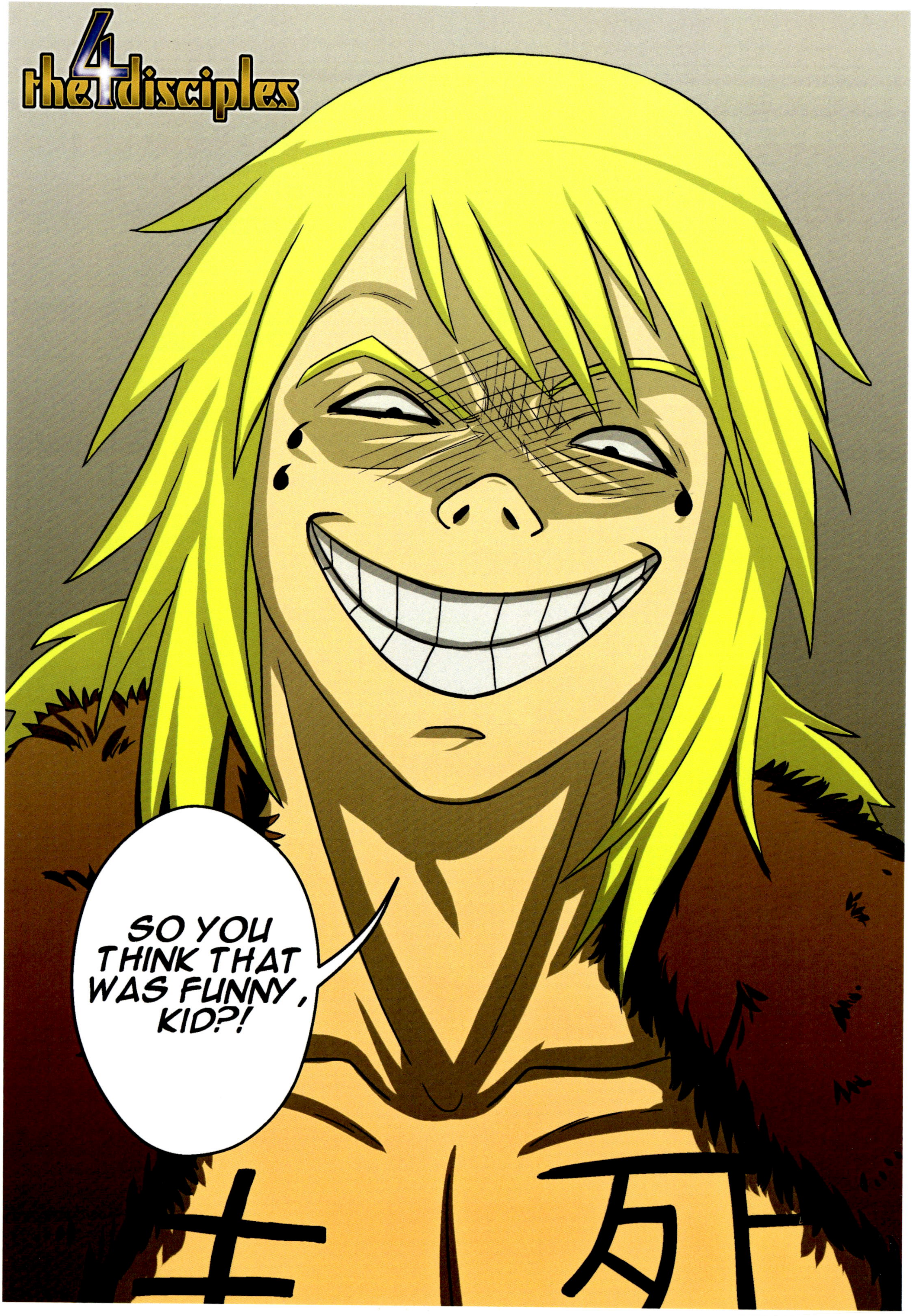
the 4 disciples
SO YOU THINK THAT WAS FUNNY, KID?!

AERON

POLICE REPORT

NAME: AERON
AGE: UNKNOWN
BIRTH CITY: TROY NEW YOUR
POWERS+ABILITIES: UNKNOWN

GANG LEADER OF
'THE FIRST EVOLUTION GANG'

the 4 disciples

Sneak Peek of

the 4 disciples

Comic Book
COMING SOON
May 30th, 2017

Continue and Read ▶

SFX: WIND BLOWING

GGGRRR...
BRO, YOU AND I BOTH KNOW, WHEN IT COMES TO SCRAPPIN, YOUR NO COMPETITION FOR ME!
CHOOO!!!
CHOOO!!!
OOOOOSSSHHHHH...
SPLAT!!!
(GREAT! HERE YOU GO WITH ANOTHER TOUGH GUY ACT.)
HOW MANY TIMES ARE YOU GOING TO HYPE YOURSELF UP JUST TO BUILD CONFIDENCE, BEFORE YOU FIGHT ME?
ARGGGHHH!!!

the 4 disciples
SHAK...
CHING!
WIND GUST SLASH!
SFX: ENERGY CHARGING UP
FWOO-OOSHH!!!
FWOO-OOSH!
FWOO-OOSH!
EXPLODE!
SCATTER!

FWOOSH
(THOSE THROWING KNIVES ARE SO DOGGONE ANNOYING!)
SUN SHOWER.... BOMBSSS!!
UHHGRRR...
FWOO-OOSH!!!
CHOOO!!!
(HE'S ACTUALLY USING HIS BRAINS FOR ONCE, INSTEAD OF JUST COMING AT ME RECKLESSLY AND RELYING ON HIS HEALING FACTOR TO MAKE UP FOR HIS MISTAKES. IF HE KEEPS THIS UP, HE JUST MIGHT POSE A THREAT.)
WE FIGHT EVERYDAY! OVER AND OVER! WITH NEITHER ONE OF US COMING OUT ON TOP!! WHY ARE YOU SO PERSISTENT ON LOSING TO ME?!
FWOOSH!!!
TURNING SIDEWARD...

SHAK...
CHING!
WIND GUST SLASH!
SFX: ENERGY CHARGING UP
FWOO-OOSHH!!!
FWOO-OOSH!
FWOO-OOSH!
EXPLODE!
SCATTER!

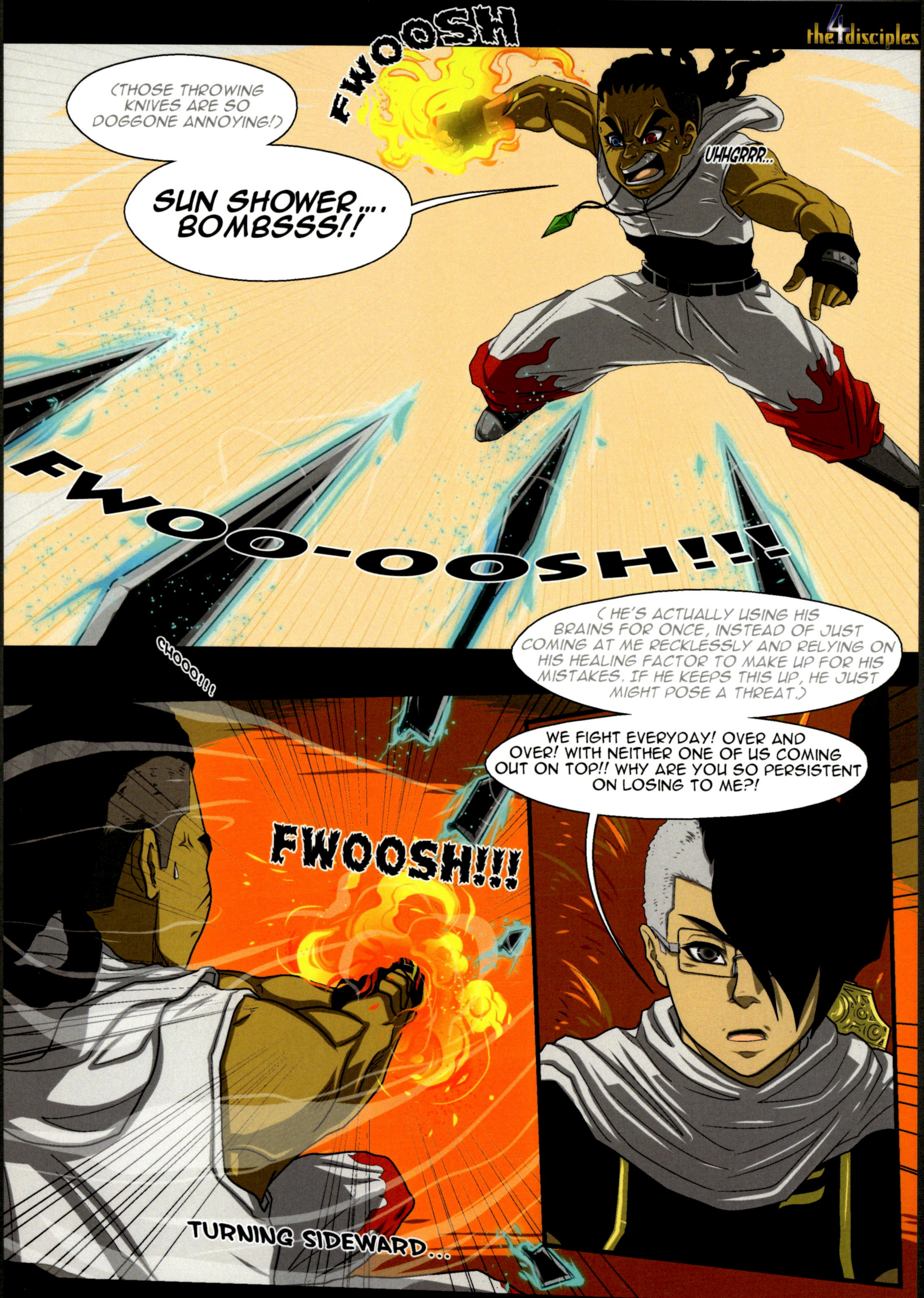

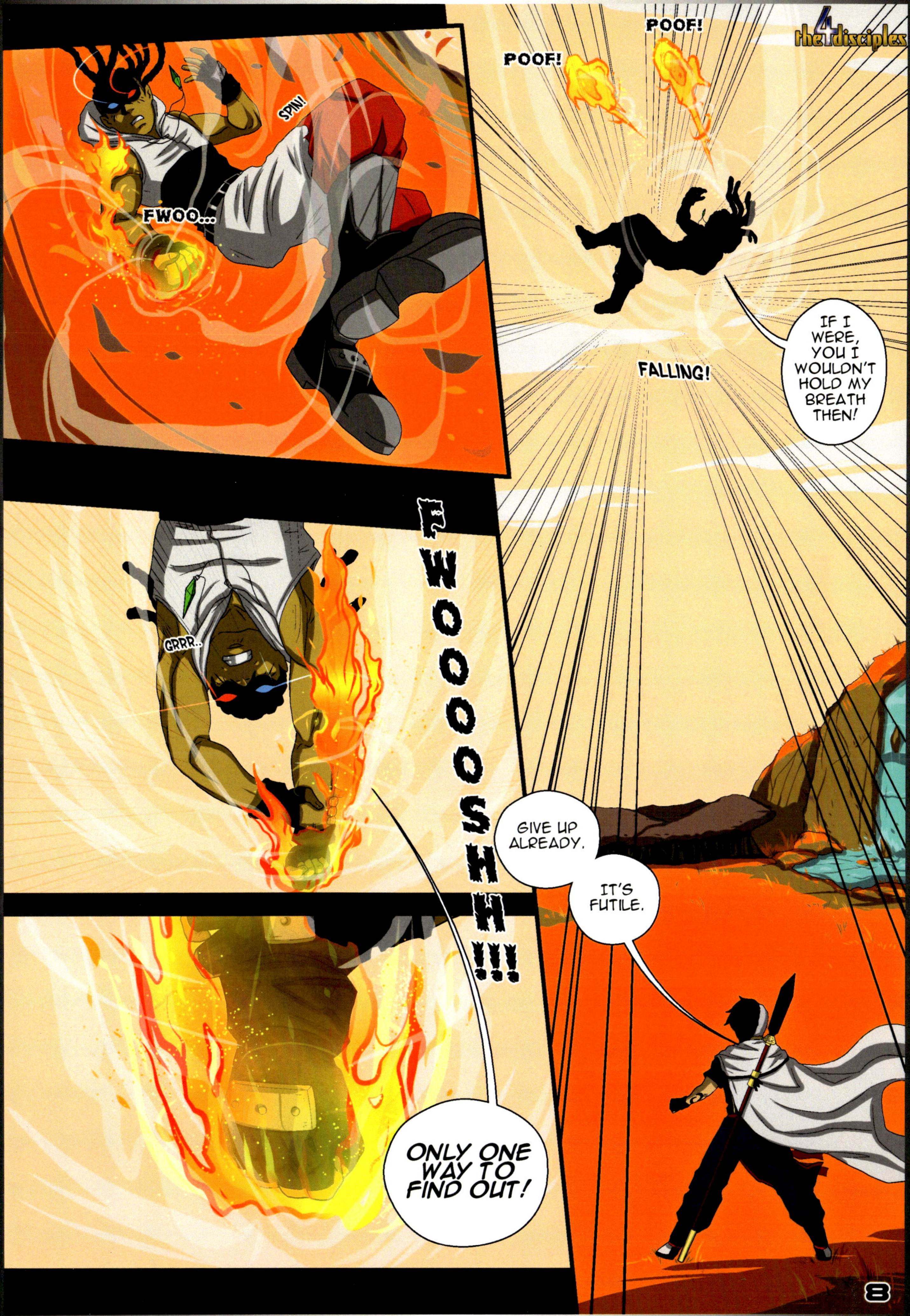
SPIN!
FWOO...
POOF!
POOF!
FALLING!
IF I WERE, YOU I WOULDN'T HOLD MY BREATH THEN!
GRRR..
FWOOOOOSHH!!!
GIVE UP ALREADY.
IT'S FUTILE.
ONLY ONE WAY TO FIND OUT!

To Be Continued...